To my husband Maurice and our wonderful children
Katee, Rachel, Mary Grace, Helen, and Patrick.

ISBN: 978-0-9886860-3-8

Library of Congress Control Number: 2015932763

Text copyright ©Diane Hoyt Voirin
Illustrations & Book Design ©Mary Gunderson
Printed in the U.S.A.
First Printing 2015

Zummy
of
Ummland

Written by Diane Hoyt Voirin
Illustrated by Mary Gunderson

Once upon a time in Ummland there lived a bear named Zummy.

Zummy was a very curious bear who loved to go exploring.

"Zummy, umm, be home for dinner!" called his mummy from the door. After waving goodbye Zummy ran out to play and explore.

First he visited one of his favorite places – Gumland!

Bright-colored pieces of gum hung from wild gumtrees everywhere! Zummy knew he was only allowed one piece of gum each trip so this time he picked a red one.

Zummy walked through Gumland into Mumland.

Mumland was a beautiful place sprinkled with pink and yellow mums. Zummy watched a Mumlandian water her flowers. She let Zummy pick a pretty pink one to take home for his mummy.

Zummy kept walking until he reached Humland. Humland was a happy place. Humlandians loved to hum tunes as they worked and played all day! Zummy smiled and hummed along with them.

Next he skipped into Drumland. Drumland was a very LOUD place where Drumlandians beat cheerful melodies on their drums all day. They waved their drumsticks at Zummy as he walked past.

After Drumland, Zummy was pleased to enter Strumland! Strumlandians played their music ever so softly and sweetly. Zummy rested a moment.

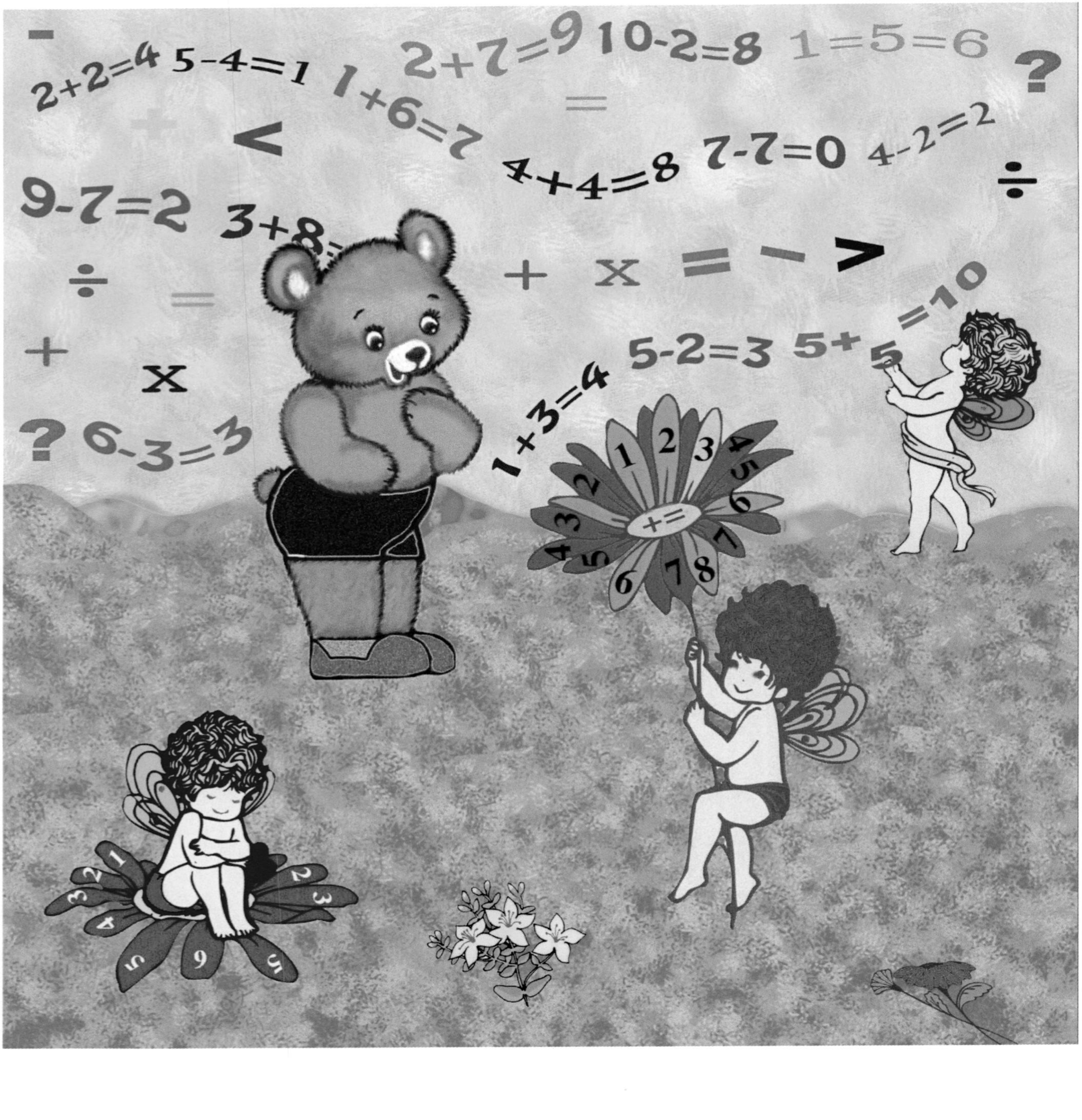
2+2=4
5-4=1
2+7=9
10-2=8
1=5=6
?
1+6=7
4+4=8
7-7=0
4-2=2
9-7=2
3+8=
5-2=3
5+5=10
1+3=4
?
6-3=3

Then Zummy entered Sumland. Sumlandians are very smart and practice their addition and subtraction tables every day. They asked Zummy what two plus two is and he quickly responded "Four!"

Zummy wandered into Chumland, a joyful place filled with friends laughing and playing two-by-two.

Just outside of Chumland Zummy realized his feet were tingling . . . which could only mean that he was in Numbland! He knew he'd best hurry along before his feet fell asleep and he couldn't keep walking and make it to . . .

Plumland! Proud Plumlandians were out picking pretty purple plums off of abundant trees. Zummy's plum-chum from school called, "Take a few back to Ummland for your mummy and your brother Jummy."

The next land Zummy entered into was Yumland. Yumland was filled with yummy treats, like the cookies and candies Mummy makes at Christmastime! Zummy's mouth watered as he passed the yummy goodies.

Zummy then scurried into Crumbland! Crumblandians live in the messiest town since they eat snacks and meals everywhere! Zummy eats only in the kitchen and dining room.

It was getting late and Zummy knew he must get home. He began walking toward Ummland but saw that he had walked all the way to Fromland! In Fromland it was easy to get lost. There were signs everywhere saying "From". "From here . . ." and "From there . . ." but there were no signs that said "To" anywhere.

Zummy was tired and scared and he knew he had gone too far.

Just outside of Fromland was Thumbland. All of the Thumblandians encouraged Zummy on. They could tell he was getting worried about making it back to Ummland before nightfall.

It was getting dark. Zummy sat down and started to cry. "Oh, how will I ever get home now?"

Just then he heard footsteps behind him. He looked up and saw his brother Jummy.

"Zummy, Mum was worried about you. You were gone an awfully long time. Did you get lost?"

"Yes, Jummy! I'm sorry! I promise to be more careful from now on."

And he was.

And they walked hand-in-hand back to Ummland.

The End

Diane Hoyt Voirin is a wife and mother who lives in Texas. She and her husband have 5 very active children. She has written newspaper articles and newsletters but Zummy of Ummland is her first book. Ms. Voirin wrote this story when she was pregnant with her first child many years ago and is delighted that her sister has illustrated it and made it a book that her children and others can enjoy.

Mary Gunderson and her husband Garry live in California, along with a few rescue kitties. Mary holds assorted offices in a few church groups and serves as a docent for Bolt's Antique Tool Museum in Oroville. She and her husband collect antique cars and are members of the Horseless Carriage Club, Northern California Regional Group. They also rescue cats and help others rescue cats and dogs.

63484619R00024